Harry

This series is for my riding friend Shelley,
who cares about all animals.

STRIPES PUBLISHING
An imprint of Magi Publications
1 The Coda Centre, 189 Munster Road, London SW6 6AW

A paperback original
First published in Great Britain in 2008

Text copyright © Jenny Oldfield, 2008
Illustrations copyright © Sharon Rentta, 2008
Cover illustration © Simon Mendez, 2008

ISBN: 978-1-84715-047-9

The right of Jenny Oldfield and Sharon Rentta to be identified
as the author and illustrator of this work respectively has been asserted
by them in accordance with the Copyright, Designs and Patents Act, 1988.

A CIP catalogue record for this book is available from the British Library.

Printed in Belgium

2 4 6 8 10 9 7 5 3 1

Harry

Tina Nolan
Illustrated by Sharon Rentta

ANIMAL MAGIC
Meet the animals

Visit our website at
www.animalmagicrescue.net

Working our magic to match the perfect pet with the perfect owner!

HARRY

Dumped in a rubbish bin, Harry is silky and soft with a sweet face, and he's very friendly! Can you resist?

HUGO

Poor Hugo was found in a box on our doorstep. Can you give him a home with lots of cuddles?

PRINCESS, POPPY AND PERCY

Three orphaned kittens with attitude! These lively bundles are purr-fect!

RESCUE CENTRE
in need of a home!

BERNIE
Shy but inquisitive, this young ferret's owner has moved away, so he needs a new home. Please help!

BENJI
Only 3 months old, Benji came to us via the RSPCA. Come and see – he could be the dog for you!

PEPPY
10-year-old Peppy's racing days are over. Now in need of TLC from a kind new owner.

HONEY AND EMILY
Nosey but irresistible, this brother and sister need a home together – with a good supply of parsley!

Chapter One

"OK, Eva, you can take Blossom off the website!" Karl and Eva Harrison were busy updating the Animal Magic website.

Eva clicked the mouse until the picture of Blossom, the black and white stray cat, came up on screen. "Cool!" she said as she pressed delete. Blossom's photo and details vanished.

"She went to live with Emma Matthews on Earlswood Avenue," Karl reported. "And the couple from Clifford came in and collected Cleo the spaniel earlier this morning, so she's gone too, plus we've had two phone calls about Hugo the rabbit, and there's a man who's interested in our gorgeous Labrador, Val—"

"Stop!" Eva cried. "I can't keep up!"

It was Saturday morning and the surgery at Animal Magic was full to bursting with people eager to adopt pets. Early summer sunshine flooded through the open windows. In the stable across the yard, Mickey the noisy donkey let everyone know he was there.

"OK, I've taken Blossom and Cleo off the website, but I still have to type details about Eddie the lizard and Peppy the greyhound. Tell me again about Hugo."

"We've had two phone calls," Karl repeated.

"Eva, could you go and take over from

Joel?" Heidi Harrison broke in. "He's out in the stables with Mickey. Tell him there's a phone call for him."

Eva nodded. She was glad to break free from the computer and the chaos in the crowded room. "Hi, Grandad!" She waved as she jogged across the yard.

"Hello, how's my favourite grand-daughter!" He waved back.

"*Only* granddaughter!" she reminded him, laughing.

He grinned and strolled on towards the house. "Come and have a chat if you get the time."

"OK, I'll try!" Eva replied.

She found Joel, Animal Magic's veterinary assistant, spreading clean straw in Mickey's stable. "Joel, Mum says there's a phone call for you – hey, Mickey, get off my jumper. It's not for eating!"

"Yum!" Joel laughed. Quickly he slipped a harness around the donkey's head and handed Eva the lead rope. "Do you want to take him out to the field?"

"Cool! Come on, Mickey," she murmured, careful now to avoid his big teeth.

Clip-clop. Mickey trotted happily across the yard, tugging Eva after him. They went out on to Main Street, then down the side lane to the fields at the back of Animal Magic. "Ee-aawww!"

"Ouch!" Eva put her hands to her ears. "Not so loud!"

The donkey's ear-splitting bray brought Guinevere, Merlin and Rosie the tiny Shetland pony, cantering up the hill.

Eva led Mickey through the gate and took off his harness. "Go play!" She watched him trot off with the three ponies. *If anyone gives Mickey a home, they're going to need earplugs!* she thought as she hurried back. She was about to head back to Reception when she remembered her grandad and made a detour into the house.

"So, Evie-Bee, how are things?" he asked, cradling a mug of tea. Eva's dad sat next to him with his own "Best Dad in the World!" mug.

"Cool, Grandad! We're really *really* busy. We just found homes for Blossom and

Cleo and maybe Hugo... Hey, I've just had a totally cool idea!"

"Uh-oh!" Jimmy Harrison glanced at his son, Mark. "Why is Eva looking at me with that mad glint in her eye?"

"She *always* has that mad glint in her eye," Mark joked.

Eva rolled her eyes and rushed on. "Grandad, why don't *you* adopt Mickey?"

"Who's Mickey?"

"Don't ask, Dad!" Mark warned. But it was too late.

"Mickey is a gorgeous donkey with long ears and ginormous eyes..."

"And a voice to match," Mark cut in.

Eva ignored her dad. "He's totally friendly and soft and cuddly, Grandad. He wouldn't hurt a fly. And you've got that big empty field behind your garden centre. There'd be plenty of room for

Mickey there. He'd love it!"

"Say no," Mark advised.

"Da-ad!" Eva was cross now. "Do you want to find Mickey a home or not?"

"Yes, but it has to be the *right* home. Don't forget how busy Grandad is. Besides, what would his neighbour say if Mickey woke them up at six every morning?"

Eva frowned. "Grandad doesn't have any neighbours," she pointed out. "Miss Eliot moved out. Ash Tree Manor is empty."

"Not any more," Jimmy told her. "A new family called Platt have just moved in. They're doing the old place up, and good luck to them."

"Oh – well, I'm sure they'd like Mickey." Eva got the feeling she was losing the argument. It seemed that Mickey would have to stay on the Animal Magic website a while longer. "Gotta dash – I promised Mum I'd help out!" she said. "But, Grandad, will you think about poor Mickey stuck here while everyone else is getting adopted? He's starting to think no one wants him!"

"Bring on the sad violins, take out your hankies!" Eva's dad sighed.

"Da-ad!" It was no good. "Bye, Grandad!" Eva said, sighing and giving him a quick hug before hurrying back to the surgery.

That morning, Animal Magic took in three orphaned kittens, a ferret, two rabbits and a grey, smooth-haired cross-breed pup called Benji. They found a good new home for Val, as well as Blossom and Cleo.

"Working our magic!" As he sat at the computer, Karl happily chanted the centre's catchphrase. "To match the perfect pet with the perfect owner!"

Heidi had finally closed the doors and stood at the desk with Joel. Meanwhile, Eva and Karl were busy uploading photos of all the new animals on to the website.

"What a morning! Thanks, everyone." Heidi took off her white coat and glanced at her watch. "Lunchtime!"

They were trooping out into the yard when Joel dropped his bombshell. "Erm, Heidi, there's something I need to talk to you about," he began awkwardly.

Heidi shaded her eyes from the sun. "To do with your phone call earlier?"

Eva and Karl turned and looked at Joel, who took a deep breath, then nodded.

"Yes, it was important."

"So?" an unsuspecting Eva asked.

Joel looked down at the ground. "It was about a new job I applied for. They made up their minds. It seems I got it."

"You want to leave Animal Magic?" Eva gasped.

"I don't want to, but I am," Joel told them. "At the end of this month, if that's OK, Heidi?"

Chapter Two

"Moscow!" Eva couldn't believe Joel's news. "It snows all the time. It's freezing. It's hundreds of miles away. Why do you want to work there?"

It was early afternoon and Joel was checking stock in the drugs cabinet. He ticked off items on a long list and tried to explain. "The job is connected with the main vet school. I'll get to work with some amazing experts. And I'll learn a lot of new stuff."

"But what about us?" Eva sprayed tables in the surgery and wiped them clean. "Anyway, you could learn new stuff from Mum."

"No, I couldn't," Joel said firmly. "I've loved every minute here, Eva, but it's definitely time to broaden my horizons and move on."

Eva knew she would miss Joel. With his tall, gangly figure and mop of light brown curls, he'd been part of the Animal Magic team since it opened. Now he felt like part of the family. "Will you still come back and see us?" she asked.

"Just try and keep me away!" He grinned, picking up the phone. "Hello, Animal Magic ... oh, hi there, Jimmy. No, Heidi and Mark have gone to the shops. Eva's here though. It's your grandad," Joel said as he handed the phone over.

"Eva, listen there's a problem here at Gro-well!" Jimmy Harrison sounded upset. "Two big dogs – Dalmatians – have escaped from next door's garden. They're making a right mess of my bedding plants."

"Oh no! Grandad, I'm sorry. Isn't anyone trying to stop them?"

"No. I've been round to the manor house but there doesn't seem to be anyone at home. I was wondering if there was someone at your place who could lend a hand?"

To get two rampaging dogs under control? You bet! "I'll find Karl. We'll cycle over straight away," Eva promised.

"Find Karl to do what?" Karl asked, wandering out of the cattery with one of the new kittens. "Where are you dragging me off to now?"

"Here, pass her to me." Quickly Joel took the grey kitten from Karl. "It's important, so don't ask questions – just follow Eva!"

Eva and Karl cycled up Main Street, out of the village towards their grandad's small garden centre.

"I've never heard him sound this upset before," Eva told her brother. "You know Grandad – he's always so..."

"Happy?" Karl chipped in.

Eva nodded. They flung down their bikes at the gates to the garden centre and ran into the tiny office to find their grandad on the phone.

"Mr Platt? This is Jimmy Harrison from the garden centre next door. Do you own a couple of Dalmatians? You do. Well, I'm glad I've got hold of you at last. Did you know your dogs have escaped from your garden? Yes, that's right. They're in amongst my plants and doing terrible damage. So I'm hoping you'll be able ... Mr Platt, are you there? Hello?"

"Don't worry, Grandad, we'll catch them," Karl promised, dashing outside.

Swiftly Eva followed him down the rows of upturned plants. "Wow, this is a mess!" she muttered.

Pots had been tipped over. Soil spilled over the narrow paths, plants lay crushed and broken. Suddenly, Eva spotted the first of the two dogs. "Over here!" she called to Karl.

The black and white spotted dog was snapping at a green hose that curled across the path. Its ears were pricked and it was pouncing as if the hose was a vicious snake.

"Down, girl. Sit!" Eva said in a stern voice.

The dog cocked her head to look at Eva, then pounced. She took the hose between her teeth and shook it hard.

Eva tried once more. "I said, down!" This time she used an arm movement that she and Karl had learned at dog-training classes. With her palm facing inwards, she crooked her forearm from the elbow and brought it up sharply towards her face. "Sit!"

The naughty dog saw her signal and obeyed.

"Good job!" Karl muttered, spying the second runaway digging a deep hole in his grandad's compost corner. He sprinted across and lunged at the dog, grabbing it by the collar.

The dog squirmed and dragged Karl down, but he held on. When he stood up, his T-shirt and jeans were covered in wet, dark-brown compost.

"Good rugby tackle!" Eva called.

"I'm too slow these days," Jimmy complained, bringing strong rope for Eva and Karl to use as dog leads. "It's a good job you two are young and nimble."

Once on the lead, the two Dalmatians seemed to calm down. Eva and Karl held on tightly as they walked them back to Jimmy's office, and commanded them to sit outside the door.

"I've lost a lot of expensive plants," Jimmy sighed, stooping to stand the nearest large pot upright. "I'll definitely need to have a serious chat with my new neighbours about this."

Just then, a short, stocky man strode in through the entrance, closely followed by a girl about Eva's age. Both had fair, straight hair and pale skin, with grey eyes.

The man spotted the Dalmatians sitting quietly outside the office. "Bonnie, Clyde – there you are!"

"Mr Platt?" Jimmy Harrison stepped forward. "We were speaking on the telephone. I think we were cut off."

The newcomer shook his head. "I was busy with something in the house so I put the phone down. But in any case, we're here now. I'm Mike, and this is my daughter, Katie."

Er, how about saying sorry? Eva thought, glancing round at the ruined plants.

But Mike Platt didn't seem as if he was the sort to apologize.

"I'd already been round to the house before I rang you," Jimmy explained. "It seemed there was nobody keeping an eye on – er – Bonnie and Clyde."

"As I said, I was busy." Mr Platt turned to his daughter. "Katie, run and see if you can spot where the dogs got through the fence."

"I've already seen the broken planks," Eva said. She turned to the girl. "I can show you if you like."

"Broken planks?" Mike Platt echoed. "Oh well, if your fence is the problem, I can't take any responsibility for my dogs getting through."

Katie said nothing and looked down at her feet.

"But that's not my fence," Jimmy objected. "It's yours."

Mike Platt folded his arms and looked him in the eye. "I think you'll find, when

you look into it, that the fence is yours,
Mr Harrison."

Cheek! Eva stared back at Katie. She
didn't like these new neighbours one bit.

"Well, there hasn't been a hole in it for
as long as I've been here," Eva's grandad
argued back. "I reckon you let your dogs
run out of control. They wrecked the
fence, then broke through and ran riot in
my garden centre!"

Mike Platt clicked his tongue. "Here, Bonnie. Here, Clyde!"

The two strong Dalmatians stood up and strained at their leads, dragging Karl and Eva off their feet and forcing them to hand the ropes to Mr Platt.

"My dogs are not out of control!" The new neighbour raised his voice.

"No way!" Katie agreed, standing up for her dad.

Eva and Karl glared at her.

"So what do you call this?" Jimmy pointed at the wrecked plants.

"Not my problem," Mike Platt said, marching off with his dogs. "If I were you, Mr Harrison, I'd replace the whole fence so it doesn't happen again."

"Yeah!" Katie muttered and followed her dad.

"Or else what?" Jimmy called after them.

"Or else you can expect a letter from my solicitor!" Mike Platt yelled back as he strode through the gates.

"So the day turned out lousy," Eva grumbled to her dad once she was tucked up in bed that night. "It was brilliant at the beginning, getting Cleo and Blossom adopted and stuff, but then Joel said he was leaving, which is totally bad news, and now Grandad finds out he's got the worst neighbours in the universe!"

"Never mind, these things happen," Mark soothed. "I spoke to Grandad and said I'd be round there tomorrow morning to help him clear up the mess. Would you like to join us?"

From under her cosy duvet Eva nodded. "Grandad was really upset."

"Yes, well it will cost him a lot of money to replace the plants and put up a new fence. And we're not even sure yet if it's his."

"Miss Eliot would never have made him do that."

"No. But she's moved out to her cosy bungalow and you have to realize that people are all different. Maybe Grandad's new neighbours won't turn out to be so bad in the long run."

"They're horrible!" Eva insisted. "Just you wait till you meet them. I'm never going to like them, Dad – I promise!"

Chapter Three

Early next morning, Heidi sat at the computer in Reception typing in the details for Joel's job. "Wanted – Veterinary Assistant. A vacancy has arisen at Animal Magic for a well qualified person to assist Veterinary Surgeon Heidi Harrison..."

"Worse luck! I wish Joel wasn't going," Eva sighed as she read the opening sentence. She glanced up and saw her dad beckoning to her through the window. "Oops, I forgot – Dad and I are going to help Grandad clear up. Is that OK?"

Heidi nodded. "Joel's due to start work soon. And Karl's around."

Eva fetched bin bags, brushes and shovels from the stables and piled them into the back of her dad's van.

"We'll soon have the place straight," Mark promised as they drove out to Jimmy's garden centre. "And if necessary we'll mend the fence so that it doesn't happen again."

As soon as they parked outside the office, Eva leaped out. "Hi, Grandad! What do you want us to do first? Shall we sweep up all the rubbish?"

Jimmy looked relieved to see them. "We've got an hour before opening time. If possible, I'd like everything straight before then."

So Jimmy, Mark and Eva set to, brushing up the spilt soil and crushed plants and tipping them on to the compost heap.

"Do you want me to save the plastic labels?" Eva asked.

"Yes please. Put them in the top drawer of the desk in my office," her grandad replied. "You'll find a whole lot of spare labels there."

"What about the fence?" Mark asked from outside the door.

Eva heard the two of them wander away discussing how it could be mended. Quickly she opened the drawer and slipped the labels in. Then she rushed outside again, eager to follow her dad and grandad.

But something made her stop. A tiny rustling noise was coming from the rubbish bin that stood by the office door. The bin was used by Gro-well customers for sweet and ice cream wrappers and other bits of waste paper. It had a domed plastic top and a flap that swung in when you tapped it.

Rustle-rustle! Eva was sure that the scrabbling noise was coming from inside the bin. "What's that?" she muttered.

Scrabble-scrabble. Maybe something was trapped in there. Something too small to climb out by itself... Gingerly Eva pushed at the flap and felt inside.

"Ouch!" She felt a sharp nip and pulled out her hand. "Ouch – ow!"

Luckily, when she looked at her finger there was no blood.

Something's in there for sure, she thought.

And it's pretty scared, otherwise it wouldn't bite. It's tiny. A mouse or a baby squirrel maybe.

With her heart beating faster, she prised off the lid of the bin and peered inside.

The bin was almost full of litter and at first Eva couldn't make out the creature that had nipped her finger. All she could see were shiny chocolate wrappers and crushed crisp packets, empty plastic bags and old newspapers. *Wait a minute!*

There was a rolled-up newspaper near the top of the pile. Two tiny black eyes peeped out of one end. There was a brown face and a pair of round pink ears.

"A hamster!" Eva breathed. "Hello! What are you doing in here?"

At that second, the hamster saw Eva and shot back down the tunnel of newspaper. Quick as a flash, Eva lifted the roll out of the bin and blocked both ends. The hamster was trapped inside.

"Dad!" she yelled. "Grandad! Come quick!"

The two men had reached the far end of the garden centre, but they came running when Eva called. "What's up?" her dad wanted to know.

"I found a hamster in the rubbish bin!" she cried. "Somebody dumped him and left him to die!"

Back at Animal Magic, Karl brushed up on hamster facts on the internet. "Syrian hamster. Sometimes known as golden hamster. Scientific name – *Mesocric* ... *Mesocricetus...*"

"*Auratus*," Joel told him. He'd just turned the rescued hamster upside down, checked and told them it was a male.

"So cute!" Eva said. "Who would dump him like a piece of rubbish? How can anyone do that?"

"Syrian hamsters can grow up to 18 centimetres," Karl reported. "There are short and long haired varieties. Colours include golden, cream, cinnamon, yellow, black..."

"This one is cinnamon banded," Joel told them confidently. "See – he has a broad white band of fur around his middle."

"Look at his little pink feet!" Eva cooed. "And his pink ears – aah!"

"Bring him a cage," Joel told her. "You'll find the right size in the storeroom outside the small animals unit. Spread plenty of wood shavings in the bottom, and make sure that you fill a water bottle for him. He's bound to be thirsty after his adventure."

"I wonder how long he was in the bin," Karl muttered.

Holding the hamster carefully in the palm of his hand, Joel gently stroked him. "He's certainly used to being handled. Nice and tame. Doesn't nip."

"Want to bet?" Eva asked as she brought back the cage. "He bit me when I first put my hand in the bin!"

"What do you expect? You'd bite too if a giant hand suddenly tried to grab you!" Karl said, grinning.

"I think he's been well looked after," Joel insisted. "So it's a mystery how he came to end up in the rubbish bin."

"Anyway, what are we going to call him?" Already Karl was planning the wording for the website entry – "Syrian hamster. Owner didn't want him. Lonely and looking for a loving home."

Eva stroked the tiny hamster with the tip of her forefinger. "He needs a cute name so people will notice him."

"Goldie," Joel suggested. "Peter, Fred, Hammy?"

But Eva shook her head. "None of those suit him."

Gently Joel lowered the newcomer into his cage and closed the door.

The hamster sat in the clean shavings. He blinked then scampered towards the water bottle.

"How about Harry?" Karl suggested.

"Harry?" As Eva tested it out, the little hamster turned his head and twitched his ears. "Harry!" Eva laughed. "He likes it. That's going to be his name!"

Chapter Four

"Dumped!" Eva insisted to Annie Brooks. She was sitting on her neighbour's fence, watching Mickey graze alongside Rosie, Guinevere and Merlin. The mare and her foal belonged to the Brookses. Rosie, the little Shetland, was staying at Animal Magic until they re-homed her, but was allowed to share the field along with Mickey.

Annie was amazed. "You mean, the hamster was just dropped into your grandad's rubbish bin and left there?"

"Left to die!" Eva frowned and shook her head. "I'm surprised the shock didn't kill poor Harry. And if I hadn't found him when I did, he would soon have starved or ended up in a dustcart! He's OK now, though. Joel checked him over and we gave him a nice comfy cage."

In the distance Mickey raised his head and let out an ear-splitting bray. The ponies kicked up their heels and galloped to a safe distance.

"So who dumped Harry?" Annie asked.

Eva shrugged. "I don't know. But I aim to find out. Do you want to help?"

Annie nodded eagerly. "Where do we begin?"

"At Grandad's place. We'll pick up the trail from the start. Right now!"

Annie jumped from the fence into her back garden. "I'll just tell Mum where we're going," she said. "Wait here. I'll be back in a second."

"You're welcome to try, but I think you've got a difficult job on your hands." Jimmy Harrison had listened patiently to Eva and Annie's plan, but now he shook his head. "It could have been any one of a hundred people who dropped the poor little thing into the bin.

I had lots of customers through here yesterday."

"I know that, Grandad, but I hoped you'd be able to remember a few details." Eva wasn't put off. She was dead set on identifying Harry's owner. "For instance, when did you last empty the rubbish bin?"

"And was there anyone hanging around yesterday who looked suspicious?" Annie added.

Eva's grandad wrinkled his nose. "Let me see now. Oh, you mean the chap wearing the black mask and the striped jumper, carrying a sack marked 'Swag' over his shoulder..."

"Grandad!" Eva groaned. "It's important. We want to find out who did this to poor Harry, and make sure they don't do it again."

"So you're turning into two young

Sherlock Holmeses." Jimmy Harrison sat down at the counter. "Now let me see. Most of yesterday's customers were people I know well – locals. I don't think any of them would be likely to abandon Harry."

"What about the customers you didn't know?" Eva asked. "Was anyone hanging about near the bin?" As she quizzed her grandad, she saw an unwelcome visitor hovering outside the entrance. It was Katie Platt, half hidden by a tall tree, but peeping round at Eva, then ducking out of sight when she realized she'd been spotted.

"Hang on a minute." Her grandad broke off to serve a customer.

"Did you see that?" Eva whispered to Annie. "Katie Platt is spying on us!"

"Katie who?" Annie hadn't heard about the new family at Ash Tree Manor.

Just then, Katie leaned back into view, but she quickly ducked out of sight again.

"That's her!" Eva hissed. "You must know who I mean. She's the new girl in Mr Hawkes's class at school."

"Oh yes, her," Annie nodded.

"What's she up to? Why is she hiding?" Eva murmured.

Annie had no time to answer before a dark-haired woman in white trousers and a bright-pink shirt appeared in the entrance.

"Come on, Katie, don't hang back. Bring

Bonnie and Clyde with you!" the woman said as she approached the counter where Jimmy had just finished serving his customer.

Reluctantly the fair-haired girl came out of hiding with the two Dalmatians. They wagged their tails and tugged Katie along, snuffling into every corner.

"Mr Harrison?" the woman said in a friendly voice.

"That's me," Eva's grandad answered curtly. He was gearing up for another argument.

"I'm Julia Platt, your new neighbour. I believe you've already met my husband Mike, and Katie, plus our two dogs."

"You could say that," Jimmy sniffed. "We didn't get off on a very good footing, I'm afraid."

Mrs Platt nodded. "Katie told me all

about Bonnie and Clyde and the damage they caused. I felt I ought to pop by to apologize."

Wow! Eva stared at Mrs Platt, then at Katie, who still looked as if she didn't want to be there.

"My husband has a lot on his mind right now," Julia Platt went on. "Our move into the manor house didn't go as smoothly as we'd hoped, and yesterday we had to deal with a broken boiler and no plumber would come out because it was Saturday – well, all I can say is that, frankly, Mike was not in the best of moods!"

Jimmy nodded. "That's all right. We won't worry any more about the incident with the dogs. We've cleared everything up and my son and I are sure we can fix the fence, no problem."

"But you must let me pay!" Where her

husband had been rude and unreasonable, Mrs Platt was sweet and helpful. "And I have to apologize again about Bonnie and Clyde's behaviour. They're young dogs, you see, and we only recently got them from an animal rescue centre in our old town. It turns out they hadn't been well trained by their previous owner."

By now Eva's grandad was nodding and smiling and the two grown-ups were getting along nicely. Only Katie Platt still looked uncomfortable as she made the Dalmatians stand by the rubbish bin, keeping them on a tight lead.

"You should talk to my granddaughter here," Jimmy was telling Julia Platt. "I'm sure Eva and her brother Karl would be able to help you with your dogs. They often retrain animals at Animal Magic, down on Main Street."

"Did you hear that, Katie?" Mrs Platt turned to her daughter. "Doesn't that sound like a good idea?"

Katie shrugged while Bonnie and Clyde pulled restlessly at their leads. They tugged so hard that Katie overbalanced and fell sideways against the rubbish bin. The whole thing toppled and fell to the ground.

Woof-woof! The startled dogs strained at their leads and broke free. They fled through the garden centre gates.

"Oh no, not again!" Katie sighed. She ran to catch Bonnie and Clyde.

"Oh dear!" Mrs Platt sighed. "I'm beginning to think those dogs are more trouble than they're worth. Only, Katie is mad about animals – cats, dogs, rabbits, hamsters, you name it."

"Really?" Eva was surprised. Katie didn't come across as the sort of kid who was mad about animals.

"Yes. Believe me, she'd be heartbroken if we let Bonnie and Clyde go."

Woof-woof! The two Dalmatians had raced next door and were rampaging down the garden.

"Come here! Sit! Lie down!" a desperate Katie cried.

"Did you say hamsters?" A sudden suspicion flashed into Eva's mind.

"Yes. Anything with fur and four legs,"

Mrs Platt smiled wearily. She got ready to lend her daughter a hand with the boisterous dogs.

"So does Katie have any other pets?" Eva asked, blocking Mrs Platt's way. "Like a hamster, for instance? Does she have a hamster?"

"Why, yes!" Julia Platt told her. Then she frowned. "Actually, no, not right now."

Yes or no? Which is it? Surely Mrs Platt must know.

"Sorry, I'd better get back next door to sort out those dogs!" Julia said as she stepped past Eva.

"What colour is Katie's hamster?" Eva called after her.

But Mrs Platt was in too much of a hurry to answer.

Chapter Five

"I bet I'm right!" Eva told Annie.

"But you can't be sure," Annie argued. Eva had been explaining her Harry theory all the way back from the garden centre.

"You must admit that it looks dead suspicious." Eva swung through the doors into the surgery where Heidi was reading through the first applications for Joel's job.

"Eva thinks it was Katie Platt who dumped Harry," Annie told Heidi.

"Uh-oh, is Eva playing detective again?"

Eva's mum was too busy to pay much attention.

"Of course!" Annie grinned. "Anyway, now she's going to let me see Harry and hold him."

"That's nice," Heidi murmured. She clicked the mouse and read some details: "Jen Andrews. Age 26, trained in Dublin, special qualification in dental nursing. Hmm."

"Here he is, right at the end!" Eva announced, leading Annie into the small animals unit. The rabbits, hamsters, guinea pigs and mice were lined up in clean, bright cages, each with a water bottle and a dish of special food.

Annie followed Eva down the row of squeaking, burrowing creatures. They passed Hugo the friendly brown rabbit up at the bars of his cage, then Honey and

Emily, two harlequin bunnies with black patches on their grey fur and black pom-pom tails. Then there were Lulu and Lucy the long-haired guinea pigs and Bernie the ferret peeping shyly out of his nest of straw.

At the end of the row Eva carefully opened Harry's cage. She reached in and picked him up.

Little Harry blinked and twitched his ears. He took a sniff at Eva's fingers and decided he was perfectly happy sitting in the palm of her hand.

"Can I hold him?" Annie asked excitedly.

Eva handed over the hamster.

His little pink feet felt funny and scratchy, his brown and white furry body was soft and warm. "Will he bite?" Annie asked.

"Not if you're gentle and don't make him jump." Harry seemed used to people,

and not easily scared, even after his ordeal
in the rubbish bin. "He's cute, isn't he?"

"Gorgeous!" Annie grinned. She pursed
her lips and pretend-kissed the hamster.
"Is he on the website yet?"

Eva nodded. "Karl took his photo and
posted him up there as soon as we'd
chosen his name."

"So, even if you're right about Katie
Platt, you don't want to send him back to
Ash Tree Manor?"

"No way!" Eva took Harry from Annie

and placed him back in his cage. Then she went to the fridge and took a slice of apple from a plastic container. "Hamster treat coming up!"

"But if Katie is Harry's real owner, shouldn't you tell her where he is?" Annie saw trouble ahead if Eva rushed on and found Harry a new home.

Eva pushed the slice of apple through the bars of Harry's cage, then shook her head. She was one hundred per cent sure that her theory was right. "Katie abandoned him, didn't she? She so doesn't want him back!"

"Even so." Annie felt uncomfortable. "I guess she might have had a reason for leaving him in the bin."

"Such as?" Eva couldn't see it. "You saw what she was like, Annie. She's just a feather-brained person who doesn't take care of her pets. That's why Harry's not going back to Ash Tree Manor."

End of story. No ifs or buts.

Back at school on Monday, Eva told as many people as possible about Harry the abandoned hamster, hoping to find him a new home.

"He's really cute and friendly," she told Miss Jennings, her class teacher. "And ever so easy to look after."

"Sorry, Eva," Miss Jennings said with a smile. "I can't possibly give Harry a home. I go away to my house in France every school holiday, and who would look after him while I was away?"

"Harry is brown and white, with furry ears and pink feet." Eva described the hamster to Mrs Owen, one of the dinner ladies at Clifford Junior. "He doesn't bite and he likes to be held."

Mary Owen stopped clearing dishes and listened carefully. "We did have a hamster once upon a time," she said.

"They're ever so easy," Eva rushed on. "You only have to clean out their cages and give them fresh water and food. If you give them a wheel to play in, that's all the exercise they need!"

Mary nodded. "I know. But my son, Matthew, is grown up now, so we don't have any pets. Besides, they make my husband sneeze if he's in the same room as them. So no, Eva, I'm afraid I can't give Harry a home."

That afternoon on the way home, Annie sympathized with Eva on the school bus. "Never mind, you tried."

Eva sighed and stared out of the window at the hedges and fields beyond. "Trying isn't enough. Honestly, Annie, I've got to find somewhere for Harry before..."

"...Before Katie Platt finds out where he is, changes her mind and decides she wants him back?" Annie guessed. "Listen, Eva, I'd ask Mum if we could have Harry, only I'm sure she'll say no."

Linda Brooks had already adopted Guinevere and Merlin from Animal Magic and was letting Rosie and Mickey graze in her field. Annie knew that asking her mum to adopt Harry would be one step too far.

As the bus pulled up at the Okeham stop, Annie and Eva piled off with the other village kids.

"George, do you want to adopt a hamster?" Eva pounced on her brother's best mate who had already given a home to Lucky the rabbit.

"Nope," he said, brushing her aside and setting off up Earlswood Avenue with mega-fanciable Emma Matthews.

Karl overheard and tutted. "I already asked George."

"Tell your mum about Harry anyway," Eva muttered to Annie as they said goodbye on Main Street.

Inside Eva and Karl's house Heidi was still going through job applications. She'd had five so far. "Which of these would you choose to interview?" she asked Karl and Eva, showing them the printouts. "Oh, by the way, I had a phone call from Julia Platt at Ash Tree Manor about Bonnie and Clyde. I told her you'd both be glad to help with dog-training classes for those two tearaways."

"You what!" Eva gasped.

"Eva, close your mouth and speak properly," Heidi told her. "It's not 'you what', it's 'pardon' if you didn't hear properly, though I'm sure you did."

"The Platts aren't Eva's favourite family," Karl explained. "But I reckon retraining the dogs would be cool. When do we begin?"

"Tonight before supper," Heidi said, still sifting through her papers. "In fact, you'd better set off now. I told Julia you'd be there by five."

"Sit!" Karl told Clyde in the field behind Gro-well. He made the arm gesture that went with the verbal command.

The young Dalmatian sat down smartly on the grass.

Click! Karl pressed the small training clicker then swiftly handed Clyde a tasty treat. Click-and-treat. It worked like magic.

Eva stood with Bonnie until Clyde had got the hang of the "Sit" command. Once, twice, three times.

"Good boy!" Karl patted the dog's broad head.

Clyde wagged his tail and licked his lips.

"Now it's our turn," Eva told Bonnie, who straight away leaped up and ran across the field skipping and jumping and acting crazy.

"Mad!" Karl sighed.

But Eva wasn't easily beaten. "Here, Bonnie!" She held up a doggie treat.

Bonnie recognized food from a long way off. Barking happily, she bounded back to Eva.

"Sit!" Eva ordered as the dog screeched to a halt. Voice and arm gesture together. Be firm. Say it again. "Sit!"

Bonnie obeyed. Click went Eva's clicker. Then the reward. Gulp! Bonnie swallowed it down.

"Again," Karl said quietly.

Eva repeated the exercise patiently and firmly. After six commands and six successes, she was happy. "Good girl!" she said, patting Bonnie. "You're a lovely dog. Yes, you are!"

Happy Bonnie loved the attention. She gazed up at Eva, waiting for the next command.

"OK, let's try 'Stay'." Karl decided. "'Sit' and 'Stay'. If Bonnie and Clyde get that far in one session they'll be doing well."

And sure enough, the young Dalmatians were smart dogs who learned easily. After half an hour of click-and-treat, Eva and Karl walked them back to Ash Tree Manor with high hopes.

"How did it go?" Julia Platt asked them, as they ushered the dogs into the utility room.

Karl let Clyde off the lead while Eva dried Bonnie's feet with an old towel.

"They did really well," Karl told Mrs Platt. "We taught 'Sit' and 'Stay'. Next time we'll try 'Come here'."

"You hear that, Katie?" Mrs Platt called over her shoulder.

As usual, Katie Platt was lurking behind the nearest large object. At her mother's urging, she edged out from behind the door.

"Bonnie and Clyde just had their first training session and they passed with flying colours!" her mum said.

Katie frowned and said nothing.

Giving Bonnie a last wipe with the towel, Eva let her go. The dog bounced off towards Katie and began to tug at the hem of her jeans. She was soon joined by Clyde and the two dogs jumped up at Katie who seemed helpless to stop them. "Down!" she ordered, but the dogs ignored her so she turned and stomped off into the house.

"I'm worried about Katie," Julia said, as if she was thinking out loud. "She doesn't seem to be settling into Okeham or her new school very well. I think she misses her old friends."

Karl nodded and blushed. There was an awkward silence.

Meanwhile, Eva's eyes wandered across the junk piled up in the utility room. There were cardboard boxes everywhere, and plastic garden chairs stacked in a corner. On top of the chairs there was a small, empty animal cage. "Hey!" Eva said under her breath.

"Well, see you tomorrow," Karl was saying to Mrs Platt.

"Yes, and thank you for agreeing to train Bonnie and Clyde. It's such a relief."

Eva double-checked the cage. It was

tipped on its end, with wood shavings spilling out through the bars. And there was a metal wheel and a water bottle and everything a hamster would need.

"Karl!" Eva ran to catch up with him out on the road. "Wait for me. Guess what I've just seen?"

"I don't know but I expect you're going to tell me."

"An empty hamster cage perched on top of the garden chairs."

"So?" Karl asked, putting on his helmet and picking up his bike.

"So that's the proof we needed about Harry. He *did* live here with Katie Platt, and no wonder she looks so guilty all the time. She so totally *is* the person who dumped Harry!"

Chapter Six

Eva's suspicions about Katie Platt had turned into concrete certainty.

"Look, it's obvious when you think about it," she explained to Annie on the Tuesday morning. "She must've already decided to get rid of Harry when she came to Grandad's garden centre with her dad. She was most likely keeping him hidden in her pocket, waiting for her chance. And when her dad was getting mad with Grandad about the fence, she happened to be standing next to the rubbish bin, so she just flipped the lid and dropped poor Harry in."

"But why?" Annie asked. She and Eva had been waiting in the dinner queue when Eva spotted Katie Platt standing alone at the dining hall door.

"Hush!" Eva warned.

"Why would Katie want rid of her hamster?" Annie whispered.

"Maybe she was fed up with looking after him," Eva suggested. "At Animal Magic we're used to people getting bored and dumping their pets – it happens all the time. They're all keen at first, then they just can't be bothered."

Annie frowned. "But her mum said Katie loved animals."

"I'm not so sure." Eva noticed Katie wander across the hall to join the queue and so she shushed Annie again.

"Stand in line," Mrs Owen told everyone, making a space for Katie behind Annie and Eva. "You're new, aren't you, dear? Whose class are you in?"

"Mr Hawkes's," Katie mumbled.

Just then Mary Owen spotted Eva. "Oh hello, Eva, I'm glad I've seen you," she said in her loud, cheery voice. "I mentioned Harry the hamster to my son, Matthew."

Eva drew a deep breath and frowned. For once she didn't want to talk about Harry – not with Katie listening.

Mrs Owen chatted on regardless. "It turns out that Matthew would be keen on having a hamster for his own little boy. He's thinking of bringing Kyle out to Animal Magic at the weekend to take a look at little Harry."

Eva nodded. *Talk about something else!*

By now Katie was taking in every word, biting her lip and looking more unhappy.

"What colour is Harry?" Mrs Owen asked, reaching behind Eva's back to get a plate for Katie.

Nightmare! Change the subject. Can't you see – I don't want Katie to know! But the dinner lady wasn't picking up any of the signals. On she went.

"And how come the poor thing ended up at the rescue centre in the first place?"

Before Eva could clear her throat to give an answer, Annie nudged her with her elbow. "Er-hum!"

Eva turned, in time to see tears welling up in Katie Platt's grey eyes.

Mrs Owen noticed too. "Oh dear!" she murmured as Katie turned and dashed out of the hall. "Was it something I said?"

"Kyle Owen". Karl made a note of the name. "You say he's coming in to see Harry this weekend?"

"I hope!" Eva told him. It was already Thursday evening and Mrs Owen had spoken to Eva again about her grandson and how keen he was to have a pet. "So keep your fingers crossed!"

"Who are we keeping our fingers crossed

about now?" Heidi had just come into Reception with a stranger – a tall, thin-faced woman with fashionable jet black hair, dressed in jeans and a red jumper.

"Harry," Eva answered. "We might have found the perfect owner."

"Matching the perfect pet with the perfect owner!" The woman obviously knew the Animal Magic motto. She smiled as she said it and her serious face was transformed. Her grey eyes shone and her lips curled to show perfect white teeth.

"Eva, Karl, this is Jen Andrews – she's applied for Joel's job so she's come to take a look around."

Eva's "hello" was guarded, but Karl shook Jen's hand. "Do you want me to show you the cattery?" he offered.

"Yes, that sounds good," Jen said,

eagerly following Karl out of Reception.

"Maybe you could show her round the small animals unit afterwards," Heidi suggested to Eva. "I've already shown her the kennels. She seems nice."

"OK," Eva agreed. But it seemed odd to be showing Jen around when Joel was still here – as if she was helping to shove him out.

"How many small animals do you have right now?" Jen asked after Karl had done his part of the tour. She was following Eva down the row of rabbits and guinea pigs towards the cage at the end.

"Twenty," Eva told her. "I like them all, but Harry is my favourite."

Jen stooped to look into Harry's cage. "Yes, he's a handsome chap," she agreed. "Can I hold him?"

Warming to the newcomer, Eva nodded.

She opened the cage and scooped up Harry.

"He's quite perky, isn't he?" Jen smiled as she handled him. "Does he have a regular grooming routine?"

Eva nodded. "His nails are a bit long, though. I'm going to ask Mum or Joel to clip them."

"Good idea." Inspecting Harry carefully, Jen's smile faded a little. "Hmm, Harry's eyes are a bit watery. Have you noticed?"

"No. Is that bad?" Suddenly Eva was anxious.

"Could be. Has Harry had much soft food since he came in?"

Eva thought for a moment. "I give him apple as a treat. Does that count?"

Jen nodded and pressed gently against the hamster's cheeks. "Sometimes soft food gets stuck way back in the cheek pouches. It presses against the tear ducts and makes their eyes water. I'm pretty sure that's what's happened to Harry."

"I didn't know that!" Eva gasped. "Poor Harry – he's sick and it's all my fault!"

"Don't worry, it's not serious," Jen said calmly. "But it makes him uncomfortable. What we need is a tiny eyedropper filled with warm water that we can drop into Harry's mouth to flush out the pouches."

Eva nodded and went quickly to the storeroom to fetch the dropper. Soon Jen was holding open Harry's mouth while Eva gently dropped in the liquid.

"There!" With her little finger Jen eased the food out of the back of the hamster's cheek pouches. "That's better, isn't it?"

Eva nodded and sighed. *What a relief!* "How come you know so much about hamsters?" she asked.

Smiling, Jen put Harry back in his cage. "I made a special study of small rodents when I was at college – especially illnesses to do with their mouths and teeth."

"Cool!" Eva stood back to watch Harry go to his wheel and climb inside. Soon he was trotting and the wheel was turning fast. "Really, Jen – thanks. Harry's totally happy now, thanks to you!"

Chapter Seven

"Jen Andrews gets Eva's vote," Heidi told Joel. It was Saturday morning and she and Joel were on the porch outside Reception talking through the applicants for Joel's job. "In fact, since Thursday she can hardly wait to shove you out of the door!"

"That's not true!" Eva yelled as she set off across the yard on her bike. "I still want Joel to stay, but if we have to have someone new, I want it to be Jen!"

"No one could ever accuse Eva of

holding back her opinion!" Heidi laughed, watching her daughter follow Karl up Main Street.

It was time for another session with Bonnie and Clyde and Eva was looking forward to it. *So long as we don't see Katie*, she thought. All week at school she'd been avoiding her, and at nights when she and Karl came to do their training sessions, Eva had been glad when Katie wasn't around.

"Don't you think you're being a bit hard on the poor girl?" Eva's grandad had asked after the Friday evening lesson. He'd been watching from his side of the fence and applauding every time Bonnie and Clyde got something right. He'd also seen Eva deliberately turn away from Katie when Julia brought her out to watch too.

"No way!" Eva had said. "Grandad, it

was Katie who dumped Harry in your bin, remember? How can I be friends with someone as cruel as that?"

Overnight Jimmy Harrison had been thinking about what Eva had said and this morning he stopped her as Karl went ahead and turned into Ash Tree Manor.

"Hello, Evie-Bee," he greeted her. "How's my favourite..."

"I'm in a hurry, Grandad!" she called. "Bonnie and Clyde will be waiting for us."

Sure enough, the Dalmatians had heard her voice and set up a duet of excited barks and yelps from the Platt's utility room.

"I just need a quick word," Jimmy said.

Oops! Eva guessed she was in trouble. "What did I do wrong?"

"Nothing," he assured her, taking off his thick gardening gloves and rolling back his sleeves. "It's not what you *have* done –

more what you *haven't* done!"

Woof-woof! Karl had opened the utility room door and the dogs rushed out.

"What do you mean?" Eva was itching to get into the field with Karl and the Dalmatians.

"You haven't made friends with Katie," Jimmy explained. "And I think perhaps you've been a bit hasty."

"Oh!" Eva frowned. She thought she'd explained all that.

Her grandfather pressed on. "Katie seems pretty unhappy," he pointed out.

Sulky – yes. Bad tempered – definitely. But unhappy?

"Think about it – she's just moved to a new house, a new school, with hundreds of new people. Her mum and dad are too busy with the house to help her settle in properly. How would you feel if you were her?"

"Grandad," Eva protested. "You missed out one big thing – Katie Platt has been cruel to Harry, remember. She dumped him and he could have died!"

There was a long pause while Jimmy

Harrison rubbed his chin. "Perhaps," he said quietly. "But you don't know for definite that it was Katie, and even so, Eva, I think you should give her a second chance."

"Sit!" "Stay!" "Come here!" Eva and Karl ran through the commands.

As usual, Bonnie and Clyde were A-grade students.

"Nice work!" Jimmy called from his rows of sweet peas and roses.

"You'd never recognize them as the same dogs!" Mike Platt praised what he saw. He'd come out of the house, dressed in paint-spattered jeans and an old T-shirt.

"What did I tell you?" Julia Platt joined him as Karl and Eva went on with the lesson. "Come and look, Katie. See how well the dogs are doing!"

Katie trailed out of the house to stare blankly over the garden wall into the field beyond.

"Now we'll do 'Fetch!'" Eva decided, setting a stick in the grass. She told Bonnie to sit and stay.

Bonnie fidgeted as she gazed longingly at the tempting stick beside her. She pricked her ears, then looked up at Eva who had walked twenty steps across the field.

"OK, good girl. Now, 'Fetch!'" Eva called.

Quick as a flash, Bonnie grabbed the stick and raced towards Eva.

"Good girl!" Click-and-treat. "Clever girl. Well done."

That afternoon Eva made a plan with Annie to saddle Guinevere and ride down to the river.

"We want to see if Guinevere likes to paddle," she told Heidi, who was busy as usual giving injections and taking temperatures. "Some horses like water, don't they?"

"Yes, and some don't," Heidi warned. "When I was young, I had a pony who wouldn't even go near a puddle." She glanced up as the door to Reception opened and Julia Platt walked in with two lively customers. "Hello, what can we do for Bonnie and Clyde?" she asked with a pleasant smile.

"We'd like you to microchip them," Julia explained, holding the door open for Katie who trailed after her as usual. "We knew when we collected them from the other rescue centre that they would need chipping."

The Dalmatians pattered around the tiled floor, sniffing the disinfectant smells and poking into every corner.

"No problem," Heidi assured Julia. "Sit down here while I get things ready in the treatment room."

"OK, Mum, I'm off to find Annie!" Eva said hastily. She didn't even glance at Katie as she left.

But she was only halfway across the yard when she remembered Guinevere's treat and she rushed back into Reception. "I forgot the apple for Gwinnie!" she called, making a dash for the storeroom outside the small animals unit.

Eva delved into a cardboard box on top of the fridge and picked out the juiciest apple. She was just heading back when she heard a movement from inside the unit. *Better check that everything's OK*, she thought, and pushed open the door.

Katie Platt had sneaked in and was tiptoeing down the row of cages, gazing in at Hugo, Honey and Emily, Lulu and Lucy and the rest. When she came to Harry's cage, she crouched down low.

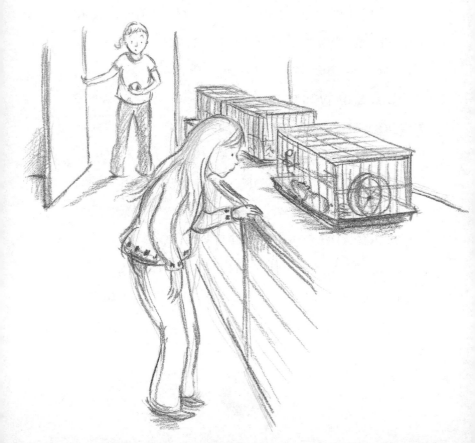

Eva watched in amazement. *How can she face him after what she did to him? What's she up to?*

Katie did nothing except stare at cuddly, easy-going Harry. The hamster came to the bars of his cage, poking his pink nose through and twitching his whiskers.

"Ahhh!" Katie said softly.

Then Heidi and Julia came to find her.

"Eva, I thought you'd gone riding," Heidi said, squeezing past.

"I am – I forgot Gwinnie's apple!" Eva gabbled.

"Ah, Katie, there you are." Julia spied her daughter by the hamster's cage. Her smile faded. "Time to go," she said sadly.

Katie's lip trembled and she put her hand up to the bars of Harry's cage. "Bye!" she whispered, following her mum back into Reception.

Chapter Eight

That evening Eva was serious and silent.

"What's up? You haven't said a word for at least five minutes. Are you sick?" Karl asked after dinner.

"Yes, sick of you asking stupid questions," Eva grumbled. Annie had said the same thing out on the ride – was Eva OK? Had something bad happened at Animal Magic?

"No, everything's cool," Eva had told her. But she couldn't work it out. Why had

Katie Platt snuck in to see Harry?

And why had she looked as if she was about to cry?

I get it! she thought suddenly as she put on her pyjamas and brushed her teeth. *Katie abandoned Harry and now she's feeling guilty! She had to make sure it was him and that he was OK. But now she's feeling really bad!*

Mystery solved. Eva went to bed feeling clearer. At least Katie Platt wasn't a total monster after all.

Eva got up next morning full of energy, with high hopes that the sunny Sunday would bring in lots of people wanting to adopt pets.

"I've got a feeling that it's going to be a good day!" she announced to Karl, who was already updating the website in Reception. "I bet we find homes for at least five of our animals."

"That would be an amazing day," Karl muttered. "In fact, you'd probably need to wave a magic wand to get five in one day."

"Huh, you're funny." *Typical Karl.* "First off, Mickey – I've decided, I'm going to ask Annie's mum to have him."

Karl grunted. "I won't hold my breath there then. Face it, Eva – Linda's more likely to adopt Rosie than Mickey."

"Linda likes Mickey!" Eva protested. "Yesterday I saw her in the field stroking him and giving him a carrot."

"Who else?" Karl challenged.

"Hugo," Eva decided. "I bet one of those people who phoned up about him comes in."

"And?"

"Harry!" she declared. "Mrs Owen's grandson will want him the minute he sees him." There was no more time to convince Karl before the first people arrived.

"We'd like a dog," a middle-aged couple explained to Joel. "We've just lost our beloved Sandy. She was fifteen. Now we're looking for a dog that's already house trained, and not too lively."

"How about Benji?" Eva broke in. "And Penny's very friendly. She's got lovely floppy ears. Would you like to look at them?"

The couple smiled and nodded. They followed Joel and Eva into the noisy kennels. Within a few minutes they'd fallen in love with Benji and decided he was the dog for them.

"Success!" Eva reported to Karl when she went back into Reception. She spotted a man and a small curly-haired boy reading leaflets in the rack while they waited. "Is your name Kyle Owen?" she asked the boy eagerly. "Have you come about a hamster? Follow me!"

The boy and his dad went with Eva into the small animals unit.

"Your granny sent you, didn't she? I told

her all about Harry. He's right at the end of the row." Talking ten to the dozen, Eva led the way.

"Wow!" Little Kyle was amazed by each animal he came to. He liked the rabbits and the guinea pigs. "They're cool. What are they?" he asked, pointing to Honey and Emily. And, "I like this one," he cried, stopping by Bernie the ferret's cage.

"Harry's down here," Eva insisted.

But Kyle was staring in wonderment at Bernie, who was sitting by the bars, raised up on his haunches, his front paws dangling. "What's his name?"

"That's Bernie. He's a ferret," Eva said.

"Look how fast he moves," he said to his dad, as the ferret darted to the back of his cage and burrowed in his straw bed. "Look – his face is peeking out."

"Do you like him?" Matthew Owen asked with a smile.

Eva frowned. This wasn't meant to be happening. But then again, it would be great if Bernie found a new home. "Erm, would you like to see Harry before you make up your mind?" she asked quietly.

"I'd like this one, Dad!" Kyle's eyes were shining. "Can I have him?"

And that was it – love at first sight. Ferret or hamster – it didn't matter to

Kyle. Matthew Owen filled in the forms and he and Kyle took Bernie home.

"Sorry, Harry," Eva said to her favourite hamster when she went back to refill his water bottle. "You're still homeless, but don't worry – I'm sure it won't be for long."

Harry ambled up and sniffed at her hand. Then he went back to his squeaky wheel and trundled. *I'm not worried*, he seemed to say. *I'm quite happy here, thank you very much!*

Chapter Nine

"Hugo is really tame and friendly," Karl was telling a woman called Martha Shaw who had come to Animal Magic with her twin daughters, Leanne and Beth.

He'd carried Hugo's cage into Reception and put it on the desk. Mrs Shaw lifted each girl to peer into the cage.

The brown rabbit flicked his long ears. He crept forward to the bars, wrinkling his nose and twitching his whiskers.

The twins smiled and giggled.

"He's lovely," they said. "Can we have him?"

"Yes, if you promise to take it in turns to feed him and clean his hutch," their mum agreed.

"And give him lots of cuddles," Eva added. She'd seen how well things were going and was hovering by the computer, ready to take Hugo off the website.

"We promise!" Beth and Leanne chorused.

So Karl and Eva gave the twins a stack of leaflets about how to take care of a rabbit while Joel took the family's details.

"Izzy-wizzy, let's get busy!" Eva cried after the Shaws had left with Hugo. She danced around the waiting area pretending to wave a magic wand. It was only three o'clock and they were having a brilliant run of luck. "Who says we can't find homes for five pets in one day!"

"Hugo, Benji, Bernie," Karl counted the names on his fingers. "Doh! That's only three."

"Someone else is coming in to visit the kennels in half an hour," she reminded him. "Mum said they were interested in a Jack Russell, and we've got Mitch."

"Which will make four, not five," Karl said stubbornly.

Eva frowned and thought hard. "Wait here!" she said, making a dash outside.

She ran next door and found Annie and her dad sitting in the sunshine. "Hi, Mr Brooks. Hi, Annie. Where's your mum?"

"Out in the field with the ponies. Why?" Lazily Annie looked up from the book she was reading.

"Nothing. Never mind. I just need to see her." Quickly Eva slipped through the Brookses' back gate into the pony field where she spotted Linda Brooks's slim figure busily pulling up weeds by the fence.

"Hi, Gwinnie, hi, Merlin!" Eva said, pausing to stroke the grey mare and foal. She gave Rosie a quick pat then put her hands to her ears as Mickey trotted up and gave his ear-splitting greeting. "Ouch, Mickey! Nice to see you too!"

The noise made Linda look up. "Hello, Eva!" She waved.

Eva jogged to join her.

"I'm digging up ragwort," Linda explained, straightening up and easing her back. "I don't want to run the risk of Gwinnie and the rest eating it."

"No way!" Eva was happy to help dig up the poisonous weed. She tugged at the roots and threw the plants into Linda's bucket. "So how are Guinevere and Merlin today?" she asked casually.

"Fine, thanks."

"And Rosie?"

"Rosie's doing fine as well. Have you found anyone who wants a lovely little Shetland pony yet?"

Eva shook her head. "No, but we will soon." She dug up another weed. "And how's Mickey?"

"Ee-aww!" The donkey kicked up his heels and cantered across the field.

"Fine." Linda Brooks looked hard at Eva. "What are you up to?" she asked.

"I'm helping you with the ragwort," she said innocently.

"No, really – I'm getting the strong feeling that you *want* something."

Eva took a deep breath then stood up straight. "OK then, I do. It's about Mickey. He's sweet, isn't he?"

"'Sweet' is not quite the word I'd use." A doubtful Linda followed the donkey's noisy progress across the field.

"But you like him?"

"I wouldn't say 'like' exactly either."

"He makes you laugh?" Eva persisted. "He's funny, isn't he? He's – interesting, clever..."

Just then, Mickey reared up at a black

and white shape that came hurtling across the field towards him. "Ee-aww! Ee-aww!"

"And noisy!" Linda sighed. "And no, Eva, before you ask – I won't adopt Mickey!"

Eva's shoulders sagged.

"But it was worth a try," Linda Brooks said with a smile.

In any case, Eva had recognized the black and white creature racing through the long grass. "Bonnie!" she called.

The runaway dog barked and swerved away from Mickey. She bounded towards Eva.

"Sit!" Eva said sternly.

Bonnie obeyed.

"You're a bad girl," Eva said, wagging her finger. "You've run away from home, haven't you?"

Bonnie gazed up with her big, dark eyes and an expression that said, *Please don't tell me off!*

"And now I'm going to have to take you back." Eva tried not to smile at Bonnie's crestfallen look. "Heel!" she told her, setting off up the field.

Good as gold, Bonnie trotted along at Eva's side.

"I'm taking you back to Ash Tree Manor," Eva told the runaway. "And I'm going to tell them to keep an eye on you in future." She talked quietly as they reached the road and turned right. "This is a busy road. You could've been run over."

The springy steps of the young Dalmatian kept pace with Eva's fast walk.

"I bet it's Katie's fault," she grumbled. "She probably left the gate open. Sit, Bonnie. Wait for this car. OK, now we can cross. Heel! Good girl – we're almost there!"

Chapter Ten

Eva took Bonnie up to the front door of the old, ivy-covered house and rang the bell. "Hello, is anyone at home?"

There was no answer so she walked round the side. "Hello?" she called again, hopefully. She was anxious to drop off Bonnie and get back to Animal Magic.

It was Bonnie who decided what to do next. She trotted towards the utility room and pushed at the half-open door.

"Good girl," Eva muttered. Honestly, the

dogs had more brains than the humans who lived here! She followed Bonnie inside, deciding that she should make sure that she had a dish of fresh water before she shut her in.

Just as Eva had filled up the metal dish, she spotted Katie Platt through the window, running up the drive.

"Have you seen Bonnie?" Katie gasped. "We were taking her and Clyde on a walk by the river, but she ran away!"

Eva stared. Katie had obviously sprinted all the way home. Her fair hair was sticking to her forehead and her face was pink. "Bonnie's here," she answered quietly. "I brought her back."

"I told Dad not to let her off the lead," Katie panted. "We were near the golf course and she ran off to chase a ball. She wouldn't come back when we called."

Eva nodded. "I caught her in the Brookses' field."

Katie pushed her hair back from her face. Then she ran to check on Bonnie. "Thank goodness!" she cried as she opened the door to the kitchen.

Bonnie bounded out and jumped up at Katie, licking at her face and leaving dirty paw marks on her T-shirt.

"Sit!" Katie pleaded. But as usual the excited dog ignored her.

"Make her do it," Eva said, annoyed that all her good training was wasted on Katie. "But do the arm movement at the same time. Like this. 'Sit!'"

This time, Bonnie obeyed Eva's command.

"You do it," Eva told Katie.

But Katie shook her head and headed out of the utility room. She began to trail back down the drive.

"Hey, stop!" Eva called. She closed the door on Bonnie and ran after Katie. "It's easy. And Bonnie's a fast learner."

"I don't want to do it," Katie insisted, her eyes filling with tears. "If you're so clever, why don't you take them both – Bonnie and Clyde – and let them live with you at Animal Magic!"

The words stopped Eva in her tracks. Then she grew angry. "That's right – send them to the rescue centre. At least this time, you're not just dumping them like you dumped Harry!"

Katie had reached the gates, but now she stopped too. She turned to face Eva. "What are you talking about?" she asked slowly.

"I said, at least this time you're not dumping them in a rubbish bin and leaving them to die!"

"What? Who's Harry?" Katie insisted.

Eva felt as if she was about to burst, she was so mad. "You know who Harry is. And don't think I can't see why you want to send Bonnie and Clyde to Animal Magic. It's because you can't handle them and you're jealous of Karl and me because we can!"

"No I'm not!" Katie's face had changed from flushed pink to deadly white. She clenched her hands into fists.

Suddenly, Eva noticed the tears that had sprung to Katie's eyes. Her own anger fizzled out and she stood puzzled in the middle of the driveway.

"OK," Katie admitted. "I haven't been any good with Bonnie and Clyde. They jump up all the time and pull when they're on the lead. It's true – I'm useless!"

Oh! For the first time Eva was stuck for words.

"I loved them when I saw them in the rescue centre, but I never knew training them would be so hard. Mum and Dad haven't had any time to help me, and I felt stupid when Mum asked you and Karl, and besides, you wouldn't talk to me at school, and I didn't know why not..."

"Stop!" Eva begged. "Are you seriously saying that you don't know what you did wrong to make me not want to be your friend?"

Miserably Katie shrugged. "I thought it was 'cos I was new and Mum says I'm too shy. I shouldn't wait for other people to make the first move."

OK, if Katie wouldn't own up to what she'd done, Eva would spell it out. "The reason I wouldn't be your friend isn't because you're new or shy – whatever! It's because of what you did to Harry."

"Who's Harry?" Katie cried again. "What are you talking about?"

"Harry is the hamster you dumped in my grandad's rubbish bin!" Eva said loud and clear. She stormed back to the utility room and pointed to the empty cage. "That's his cage, as if you didn't know!"

Katie followed Eva's pointing finger with a look of horror. "That's not Harry's!"

"Of course it is – stop pretending!"

"It's not," Katie insisted with a catch in her voice. "That cage belonged to Daisy."

It was Eva's turn to take a step back and look shocked. "W-w-who's Daisy?"

Katie swallowed hard. "Daisy was my silver grey hamster. She was only six months old. But she died just before we moved house. I buried her in a little grave in the garden."

Chapter Eleven

Eva left Ash Tree Manor in a daze. She walked next door into her grandad's garden centre.

"Hello, Eva!" Jimmy came out from his office, took one look at her pale face and took her inside. "Tell me," he invited.

"Grandad, I've done something awful!" She felt the tears well up and did nothing to try and stop them.

"Is this to do with Katie Platt and Harry?" he asked gently.

Eva nodded. "I've made her really upset and it was totally my fault."

And she told him about the dreadful mistake she'd made, and how she'd shouted and made Katie cry, all because she'd thought Katie had been cruel to Harry. "It turns out it wasn't Katie after all," she sobbed. "It was someone else who dumped him!"

Her grandfather put his arm around her shoulder. "Ah, I see!"

"I'm so horrible, Grandad. Katie had to bury Daisy in a grave at her old house, and she misses her so much!"

"Yes," he said. "You were hasty, Eva. That's the way you're made. Did you say sorry?"

Eva nodded. "But 'sorry' isn't enough. I still feel rotten."

"But in another way you've helped Katie," her grandad pointed out. "You and Karl have spent a lot of time training her dogs. They're much better than they used to be, and improving every day."

Eva nodded. "And we could carry on doing that – if Katie wants us to. Or wants *me* to. Karl could carry on working with Bonnie and Clyde, no problem – *he* hasn't done anything to upset her."

Jimmy let her sit for a while. "You're not a horrible person, Eva. You just jumped to the wrong conclusion and now you've tried to put it right. From now on things will be different between you and Katie."

"I hope..." Eva sniffed. She stood up and gave herself a shake. "You're right!" she said more firmly. "Things will be different. Thanks, Grandad, I've got to go."

"Four!" Karl reported when Eva got back to Animal Magic. "A man called Tony Watson came and offered Mitch a home. He's already got two Jack Russells and Mitch has gone to live with them."

"Four," Eva sighed wearily. She went and sat behind the reception desk.

Karl stared at her. "What's up with you?"

"Nothing." For a while she fidgeted and pretended to tidy up the stacks of leaflets. Then she jumped down from her stool and shot off into the small animals unit.

"Hi, Harry," she murmured when she reached his cage.

For a while Harry kept out of sight behind a mound of wood shavings. Then he crept out and Eva spotted his sweet brown face. He peered at her with his button-bright eyes.

"So we'll never know who dumped you, Harry," Eva began in a gentle, serious voice. "And to be honest, I wish I'd never tried to find out. I mean, what does it really matter as long as we find you a lovely new home?"

Little Harry cocked his head to one side. *That's right – what does it matter?*

"Someone will love you," Eva promised, putting her face right up to the bars of his cage. "Sooner or later we'll find you the perfect owner!"

"Where's Mum? I need to give her a message!" Eva had made up her mind and dashed back out into Reception.

"What message?" Karl asked.

"Here, let me write it down." Eva scribbled a note and pushed it towards him. "No time to explain. Just make sure Mum gets this and does what it asks. I'm in a hurry. I have to spring-clean Harry's cage!"

It was five o'clock – time for Animal Magic to close its doors – when Julia Platt arrived with Katie.

Heidi stood with Karl and Joel behind the reception desk. "Ah Julia, I'm glad you got my phone message," she said with a mysterious smile. "Eva's in there waiting for Katie."

Julia whispered in Katie's ear and sent her by herself into the small animals unit.

Katie looked nervous. She glanced at the two harlequin rabbits, and Lulu and Lucy. Then she moved on down the row.

"Hi, Katie," Eva said quietly. She stood by Harry's cage with its fresh shavings, its full water bottle and little treat-dish full of chopped carrot.

Katie relaxed as she drew close to the cage. "Hi!" she replied, getting as close to Harry as she could. "You're pretty. You look lovely and soft."

"Would you like to hold him?" Eva offered.

Shyly Katie opened the cage and lifted Harry out. "Soft and silky," she murmured. "He's gorgeous!"

Little Harry twitched his nose and looked up at Katie.

"Mum thinks he's probably only about three months old," Eva said. "But he's really tame and nice to handle."

"Yes." Katie's face was bathed in smiles.

"So I was wondering," Eva began.

Katie caught her breath and looked up at Eva.

"Since you already know how to look after hamsters, and considering my mum has rung your mum to ask if it would be OK – I was wondering if you'd like to give Harry a home?"

"She said yes!" Eva carried Harry's cage and led Katie back to Reception. Both girls wore beaming smiles.

Joel was already filling out the form. "Harry," he wrote in the space requesting the adopted pet's first name. "Platt" he wrote in the space asking for the surname.

"What's Harry's favourite treat?" an excited Katie asked Eva.

"Apples, but not too much. And if he's sleeping, don't try to pick him up."

Katie nodded. "I used to whistle to Daisy and she'd come to the front of her cage. Do you think I can teach Harry to do that?"

"Yes, cool." Eva couldn't tell who was happiest – herself, Katie or Harry. "Make that five!" She grinned at Karl, who was taking Harry's name off the website. *Five rehomings in one day!*

"And you can come and see Harry whenever you like," Katie told Eva.

"Tomorrow?" Eva asked in a flash. She held the door open for Julia Platt to carry the cage out to the car. "What time?"

"I'll see you at school to arrange it," Katie promised, running ahead to open the car door.

Five! Hugo, Benji, Bernie, Mitch and, best of all, Harry! Eva waved goodbye to Katie as her mum drove off.

And now her dad was crossing the yard, coming towards the surgery with a person Eva recognized – a dark-haired woman – oh yes, Jen Andrews!

"Meet our new assistant," Mark announced. "Your mum finally made up her mind. Jen's going to replace Joel."

"Welcome to Animal Magic!" Heidi smiled at Jen, standing in the doorway with Joel, Karl and Eva beside her.

"Yes, and good luck," Joel added as he shook Jen's hand. "You'll need it if you're going to work with this animal-mad family!"

Jen nodded then took a deep breath. Her eyes settled on Eva's happy face and she smiled. "I have a good feeling about this place," she said. "I'm sure I'm going to be very happy here!"

Collect all the books in the
Animal Rescue series!

Visit the Animal Magic website:
www.animalmagicrescue.net

And look out for the next book in the series!

Barney

The baby hedgehog

When Eva finds a baby hedgehog in a nearby barn, she and Karl contact a specialist hedgehog rescue centre to find out how to look after it. Meanwhile, the search is on to find Barney's family, who unbeknown to Eva, are also in need of rescuing!

And watch out for Animal
Rescue's Christmas title!

The doorstep puppy